Dear Parent:
Your child's love of reading starts here!

Every child learns in a different way and at his or her own speed. Some go back and forth between reading levels and read favorite books again and again. Others read through each level in order. You can help your young reader improve and become more confident by encouraging his or her own interests and abilities. From books your child reads with you to the first books he or she reads alone, there are I Can Read Books for every stage of reading:

SHARED READING
Basic language, word repetition, and whimsical illustrations, ideal for sharing with your emergent reader

BEGINNING READING
Short sentences, familiar words, and simple concepts for children eager to read on their own

READING WITH HELP
Engaging stories, longer sentences, and language play for developing readers

READING ALONE
Complex plots, challenging vocabulary, and high-interest topics for the independent reader

ADVANCED READING
Short paragraphs, chapters, and exciting themes for the perfect bridge to chapter books

I Can Read Books have introduced children to the joy of reading since 1957. Featuring award-winning authors and illustrators and a fabulous cast of beloved characters, I Can Read Books set the standard for beginning readers.

A lifetime of discovery begins with the magical words
"I Can Read!"

Visit www.icanread.com for information
on enriching your child's reading experience.

The Berenstain Bears Down on the Farm copyright © 2006 by Berenstain Bears, Inc. All rights reserved. Printed in the U.S.A. No part of this book may be used or reproduced in any manner whatsoever without written permission except in the case of brief quotations embodied in critical articles and reviews. For information address HarperCollins Children's Books, a division of HarperCollins Publishers, 195 Broadway, New York, NY 10007. www.icanread.com

Library of Congress catalog card number: 2005018675
ISBN-10: 0-06-058351-7 (pbk.) — ISBN-13: 978-0-06-058351-4 (pbk.)
ISBN-10: 0-06-058350-9 (trade bdg.) — ISBN-13: 978-0-06-058350-7 (trade bdg.)

19 20 LSCC 30 29 28 27 26 25   ❖   First Edition

The Berenstain Bears
DOWN ON THE FARM

Stan & Jan Berenstain

HarperCollinsPublishers

"This way, please.
We are on our way
to visit our friend
Farmer Ben today.

"There's Ben's farm
just up ahead.
As you can see,
it is quite a spread.

"There's Ben himself
feeding his stock—

and there's Mrs. Ben
feeding her flock.

"And there's Big Red,
the rooster,
making much ado
about his big, loud
cock-a-doodle-doo."

9

"Your farm is so big," says Ma,
"as big as can be!
It reaches as far
as the eye can see."

"Yes, it's a big 'un!"
says Ben.
"A hundred acres—
that's ten times ten.

"We grow peas and beans,

and corn and wheat,

and all kinds of other
good things to eat.

"But we have help—
Shep, our sheepdog,
herds our sheep.

"I cover a lot of ground
in my trusty Jeep.

"My scarecrow keeps
the crows away,

and, of course, farm
machines are here to stay.

"Our barn cat, Burt,
keeps the mice away.

"As for milking—I still like to do it the old-fashioned way.

"Here, Brother Bear.
Give it a try."

Oops! Brother gives Papa
a squirt in the eye.

"I have a question,"
says Sister Bear.
"What is that tall thing
over there?"

"It's the silo," says Ben,
"where we store the wheat
that we sell to folks
who make things to eat.

"Because wheat's what it takes

to make the flour   that goes into bread,

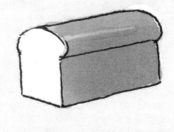

cookies,   and cakes."

Says Mrs. Ben, "It's lunchtime!
Please take your seats.
Everyone sit down
and have some eats!"

And what a lunch it is!
Farm-fresh foods
of every kind.
For dessert, they munch
watermelon down to the rind.

But Brother has another
question to ask.
"We can see that farming's
a very big task.
My question is this:
Is farming hard
or is it fun?"

"Hmm," says Ben.
"Is farming hard
or is it fun?
Well, it's not a job
for everyone.

"There are hogs to slop,

24

horses to feed,

fences to mend,

gardens to weed,

sheep to shear,

fertilizer to spread.

"But when the sun goes down
and the sky is red—
when the livestock are all
bedded down and fed,
and I sit on the porch
with Mrs. Ben—

"Er, what was that question of yours again?

"Oh yes: Is farming hard or is it fun?

31

"Well, yes, it is hard,
but we love it, son,
so I guess you might say
farming's *hard fun*."